POCAHONTAS

Based on Disney's
full-length animated movie

Hippo

Scholastic Children's Books,
7–9 Pratt Street, London NW1 0AE, UK
a division of Scholastic Publications Ltd
London ~ New York ~ Toronto ~ Sydney ~ Auckland

Published by Scholastic Publications Ltd, 1995

Copyright © Disney 1995

ISBN 0 590 13248 2

Typeset in Plantin by Contour Typesetters, Southall, London
Printed by Cox & Wyman Ltd, Reading, Berks

10 9 8 7 6 5 4 3 2

LIST OF COLOUR PLATES

1 Pocahontas, the beautiful daughter of Chief Powhatan, makes her way through the peaceful forest surrounding her village. Meeko the racoon tags along.

2 After a long voyage, the *Susan Constant* arrives in Virginia. The Englishmen aboard hope to find gold in the New World.

3 Pocahontas is intrigued by the strange visitors who have come ashore.

4 Ratcliffe, the greedy governor of the New World expedition, orders his men to dig for gold.

5 Captain John Smith scouts the terrain for natives.

6 Fascinated by the blond-haired, blue-eyed stranger, Pocahontas secretly follows Smith.

7 John Smith senses that he is being followed.

8 As Smith takes aim with his musket, he is shocked to discover Pocahontas, the most beautiful woman he has ever seen.

9 Despite their cultural differences, Pocahontas and John Smith fall in love.

10 Pocahontas teaches Smith that he must respect the earth and all its creatures.

11 Provoked by Ratcliffe and the settlers, Powhatan's warriors prepare to attack.

12 After seeing her best friend with John Smith, Nakoma worries that Pocahontas is in danger.

13 As tension mounts between the settlers and the Powhatan people, Thomas searches for John Smith, who has mysteriously disappeared.

14 Blamed for Kocoum's death, Smith is captured by Powhatan's warriors and sentenced to death.

15 Pocahontas sneaks in to see John Smith one last time.

16 Powhatan raises his club, preparing to kill Smith. Within seconds, Pocahontas will save Smith's life.

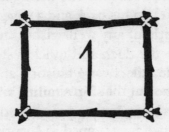

It began in old London town in the year 1607. Early one morning, the docks bustled with men loading cargo. The good ship, *Susan Constant*, was about to set sail. She would be carrying daring Englishmen on a sailing voyage far across the sea, all the way to Virginia. In the New World, the men hoped to find plenty of gold and jewels.

Thomas' whole family had gathered to say goodbye and wish him well.

"Godspeed, Laddie," said his father, shaking his hand.

"My dear boy, take care of yourself," his mother told him. She tried hard to hold back her tears.

His little sister tugged at his sleeve. "Watch out for the Indians!" she warned him.

Thomas' mother began to sob.

"Don't worry, Mum," he said, hugging her. "I'll be all right." His eyes were shining and bright. "I'm off on a great adventure!"

Not far from Thomas, another young man headed towards the ship. He was tall with golden hair. He carried a musket on his back and a silver sword at his side. Alone, without any well-wishers to see him off, he strode onto the dock and quickly stepped onto a cannon that the sailers were hoisting aboard.

Two men stood at the ship's railing and watched as the cannon was being lowered onto the deck. Lon, the shorter of the two men, gaped in surprise.

"Ben, look!" he said, eagerly nudging his companion. "Is that Smith?"

"It certainly is," answered Ben. "That's the old sea dog. Overhearing the conversation, Thomas quickly made his way over to Lon and Ben.

"Did you say Smith? Captain John Smith? I've heard some amazing stories about him. Is he really coming on this voyage with us?"

Ben rolled his eyes at Thomas' ignorance.

"Don't be a ninny," he told him. "Of course he's coming. You can't fight the Indians without John Smith!"

John Smith heard Ben and smiled. "That's right," he said. "I'm not going to let you boys have all the fun."

Down below, the crowd roared as a coach pulled up to the dockside. One of Thomas' brothers pointed to the shining gilt carriage. "Look at that!" he shouted as the team of high-spirited horses pranced up to the ship. "Must belong to somebody rich."

"Hush, lovely, mind your manners," said his mother. "That's John Ratcliffe, the Lord Governor. He's in charge of the expedition."

Governor Ratcliffe puffed a bit as he descended from the carriage, then paused to catch his breath. A skinny man hopped out of the coach right behind, carrying a little pug dog on a satin pillow with great care.

The governor strutted through the crowd with his nose in the air. The little pug rode up the gangplank right beind, his snout high in the air as well.

On deck a young man hoisted up the British flag. It snapped in the brisk wind.

"All hands on board!" he shouted.

Thomas' family waved their final goodbyes as the crew slipped the mooring ropes from the dock. The *Susan Constant* was on its way at last. As the ship floated down river, the departing men waved back to their friends and relatives. But one man did not. With his musket slung over his back and his sword at his side, John Smith faced the open sea.

For weeks the ship rolled through a calm sea, but one night the wind quickened. The huge sails billowed out and the ship charged through the tumbling waves. Lightning cracked and flashed.

3

With thunder booming in their ears the men struggled to keep the ship on course.

"Cut her speed!" ordered the captain. "Furl the sails!"

High above, John Smith swung from rope to rope, helping to secure the ship's rigging. Thomas, with panic rising in his voice, yelled up to him, "John! The cannons are breaking loose!"

John swung down from the mast and landed next to Thomas.

"Reef the topsails!" he shouted to the men. "Steady on your course!"

"It's all right, Thomas," he said. "We'll get them tied off. Don't you wor . . ."

The deck heaved as a gigantic wave exploded over the rail.

"Thomas!" shouted John. "Watch out!"

But his warning came too late. The wave sent Thomas sprawling across the deck, over the rail and into the sea.

"Man overboard!" shouted one of the men.

"Help!" Thomas yelled thrashing about in the foaming water. "Help!"

"We'll never be able to save him!" shouted Ben. "He's lost!"

As the horrified men watched, Thomas slipped further and further from the ship.

John hastily tied the end of a rope around his waist.

Then he dived over the rail.

"Smith!" shouted Ben. "Are you crazy?"

With steady and powerful strokes, John swam through the rolling waves. He reached out and grabbed Thomas.

"Hang on, I've got you!" he said, wrapping one arm around Thomas.

The men began to pull on the rope tied to John's waist.

"Harder!" Lon shouted to them. "Put your backs into it!"

Fighting against the strength of the sea, the men slowly hauled John and Thomas in. Straining every muscle, they pulled the two men alongside and hoisted them over the rail.

John and Thomas lay flat on the deck, gasping for air. The other men gathered silently around. A few moments later, John blew a stream of water out of his mouth. "That was refreshing," he said.

"Well done, Smith," said Lon. His eyes shone bright with tears of relief.

"Of course," John said looking at Ben, "I expect you'd do the same for me."

Ben gulped. "Of course. I would, sir," he stammered. "Right-o. Anytime!"

"Trouble on deck?" asked Governor Ratcliffe, coming up on deck from his cabin. Wiggins teetered behind, trying to hold an umbrella over his master's head.

"Thomas fell overboard, sir," John answered him.

Thomas struggled to his feet. "Smith rescued me, Sir."

"Thank heavens you've been successfully retrieved. Good job, Smith," the Governor said, eyeing both men. Then he raised his voice for everyone to hear.

"Don't lose heart, men! It won't be long before we reach the New World," he told them. "Just remember what awaits us; Freedom! Riches! Gold!"

Ratcliffe maintained his balance in the whipping wind.

"You are the finest crew England has to offer," he shouted. "And nothing, not wind or rain, not even a thousand Indians, shall stand in our way!"

Then he turned back towards his cabin, where it was warm and dry. Wiggins stumbled alongside still struggling with the umbrella.

"That was a stirring oration, sir," he said, opening the cabin door for him.

Governor Ratcliffe grinned. "Let us hope so," he answered under his breath. "I'll need those witless peasants to dig up my gold, won't I?"

Back up on deck, Thomas smiled at John. "This New World's going to be great. I'll get rich and build myself a big house. And if any Indian tries to stop me . . . I'll shoot him!"

John smiled back. "Just worry about that fortune of yours, Thomas. Leave fighting the Indians to me."

"Do you really think they'll give us much trouble?" Thomas asked.

Ben picked up Thomas' dripping hat and handed it to him.

"Not as much trouble as Smith'll give them!" he said.

Thomas wrung out his hat. "I never realized the voyage would be so hard."

John grinned. "You should have been on my *last* voyage!"

"Why do you keep doing this time and again?" asked Thomas.

John peered off towards the horizon. The storm had passed and the first light of dawn brightened the sea.

"I don't know, Thomas," he answered. "I suppose I never had a reason to stop."

Far across the sea, a wide river wound through a wooded land. Along its reedy shallows, marsh birds probed for tiny crabs. Further out, bluefish and flounder swam. In the deepest waters lived the giant sturgeon, each one as heavy as a small boat.

A village lay in the shady forest alongside the river. At its centre, stood a circle of wooden posts, each carved with a face. Here, the villagers often held dances. Their dwellings were made from poles and woven mats. They looked like big overturned bowls underneath the trees.

One day the village women were out in the field picking squash, beans and corn. Not far away, other forest dwellers were also taking gifts from the generous land: at the edge of the woods, white-tailed deer grazed on fern and grass; and in the thorny thicket, birds and black bears nibbled on nuts and juicy berries.

Two small children dashed from the river into the

field. "The warriors are coming home!" they called out.

The women dropped their baskets and ran to the water's edge.

Kekata, the tribal medicine man, was already there, waiting patiently. As the warriors beached their canoes, he stepped forward to welcome the Chief.

"Chief Powhatan," he said. "We have received word of your victory. Your return has brought joy to the village. Look at all the smiling faces.

Powhatan looked over the small crowd. "There is one smiling face I don't see," he said. "Where is my daughter?"

"You know Pocahontas," he answered with a grin. "She goes wherever the wind takes her. But do not worry; I sent Nakoma after her."

Nakoma paddled along the coast line looking for Pocahontas. Finally, she spotted her friend at the edge of a high cliff. With the wind ruffling her hair, Pocahontas stood gazing across the land and water that stretched before her.

As always, Pocahonatas's companion, Meeko the raccoon, was at her heels. Hovering close to her shoulder was another friend, a tiny hummingbird called Flit. Pocahontas saw Nakoma and waved down to her.

"Your father's back!" Nakoma called. "Come down here!"

Pocahontas stood poised on the edge of the cliff. Slowly, she raised her arms.

"No! Not that way!" Nakoma cried out.

Pocahontas hardly made a splash as she dived gracefully into the deep water.

Nervously, Nakoma peered down into the water.

"Pocahontas?" she said. "Pocahontas? You'd better be all right, because I'm not—"

Suddenly, the canoe tipped over and Nakoma was thrown head-first into the water.

"Pocahontas!" she laughed as her smiling friend bobbed up next to her under the overturned canoe.

"Don't you think we're getting a little old for these games? What were you doing up there?"

"Thinking," said Pocahontas.

"Oh, about that dream again?" asked Nakoma.

"I know it means something," said Pocahontas. "I just don't know what."

"Well," said Nakoma, "now that your father's back, you should ask him about it."

Pocahontas smiled. "Maybe I should."

Pocahontas and Nakoma paddled back home. As they pulled the canoe up onto the shore, Chief Powhatan was speaking to the excited villagers.

"*Chesk-cham-ay!* My friends!" announced Chief

Powhatan. "The Massawomecks are defeated. Our village is safe again."

He turned to a young warrior standing close by.

"Our warriors fought with courage," he told his people, "but none as bravely as Kocoum. Tonight we will feast in his honour."

As the crowd cheered, the young warrior stood grim-faced and still as stone.

"Kocum is very handsome," Nakoma whispered to Pocahontas.

"I especially love the smile," Pocahontas whispered back.

She started towards her father. She felt proud and happy as she pressed her way through the crowd. Chief Powhatan was loved and respected and she knew she was closest to his heart.

Chief Powhatan smiled when he saw Pocahontas. He held out his arms. "My daughter."

"Father!" said Pocahontas, holding him close to her. "I'm so glad you've come home safely."

"Come with me," said Powhatan. "Let us walk together. Tell me what you have been doing."

"Father," Pocahontas told him, "something has happened lately that I do not understand."

Powhatan touched her gently on the shoulder. "I am here to listen."

"For many nights now," Pocahontas explained, "I've been having the same dream. I think it is telling me something is about to happen. Something exciting."

Her father smiled at her. "You are right, my dear daughter," he said. "Something exciting *is* about to happen."

"Really?" asked Pocahontas. "What is it?"

With great pride in his voice, Powhatan told her, "Kocoum has asked for your hand in marriage."

Pocahontas was shocked. Marry Kocoum?

"But, Father," she said, "Kocoum is always so . . . serious."

"He is my bravest warrior, Pocahontas," said Powhatan. "I told him, if he were your husband, it would make my heart soar."

Pocahontas tried to explain her wishes.

"I think my dream is telling me something else," she said. "I think it's pointing me down another path."

Powhatan shook his head sternly.

"*This* is the right path for you," he told her. "You are the daughter of a chief. It is time to take your place among our people."

"But Father," said Pocahontas. "Why can't I . . ."

"You have your mother's spirit and independence, Pocahontas," her father continued. "You guide your canoe with ease through roughest waters. You follow tracks through the forest as well as any of my warriors. You do many things on your own.

"But even the wild mountain stream must someday join the big river, my daughter. Rivers are steady. Steady as the beating drum. Steadiness is good for people, too."

He placed a necklace around her neck. Hanging from it was a smooth white shell.

"Your mother wore this for our wedding," he said. "It was her great wish that you would wear it at your own."

He stepped back and looked at it.

"It suits you," he said, looking pleased.

Then he walked away leaving Pocahontas alone with her thoughts.

Pocahontas sat by the riverbank deep in thought. Meeko ambled down to her side, and Flit hovered over the flowers nearby.

Pocahontas thought about what her father had said. She had always followed his wishes, but this time was different. She did not want to marry Kocoum.

As she stared into the flowing water, Meeko sat quietly pawing at the water. All of a sudden, a frog shot up right under his nose! Meeko jumped back in surprise and scrambled onto Pocahontas' shoulder.

"See!" laughed Pocahontas. "Rivers aren't steady at all. They're always changing."

And who wanted to be steady, she thought to herself – steady as the beating drum?

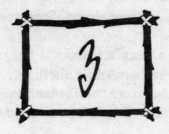

Pocahontas pushed her canoe into the water and picked up Meeko, who was nosing about for frogs.

"Come along," she said to the little raccoon. "Maybe Grandmother Willow will tell me what to do."

Whirring frantically, Flit darted out from the trees.

Pocahontas laughed. "Don't worry," she said. "We wouldn't leave you behind."

She paddled along a winding stream that flowed into the heart of the forest. Then she floated into a secluded glade. And there, as always, Grandmother Willow was patiently waiting. For hundreds of years she had stood, her deep roots drawing water from the stream and her long, trailing leaves breathing life from the sun.

Pocahontas climbed out of her canoe and sat quietly at Grandmother Willow's roots.

"Grandmother Willow," she said, "I need to talk to you."

The bark on the ancient tree began to change shape. The face of an old woman appeared.

"Good morning, Child," said Grandmother Willow, her gentle voice filling the air. "I was hoping you'd visit today. Why, you're wearing your mother's necklace!"

"That's what I wish to speak to you about," said Pocahontas. "My father wishes me to marry Kocoum."

"Kocoum?" said Grandmother Willow. Her face scrunched into a frown. "But he's so . . . serious."

"I know," said Pocahontas. "Father thinks it's the right path for me. Pocahontas stroked Meeko's back. But there's something else. Lately, I've been having a strange dream."

"Oh good!" interrupted Grandmother Willow. "You know how I love dreams! Tell me about it."

"I dream," Pocahontas began, "that I am running through the woods. Then right there before me, is an arrow. As I look at it, it begins to spin."

"A spinning arrow!" said Grandmother Willow. "How unusual."

"Yes!" agreed Pocahontas. "It spins faster and faster, until suddenly, it stops."

"And then?" asked Grandmother Willow.

Pocahontas shrugged her shoulders. "And then I wake up."

Grandmother Willow was silent for several minutes.

"Hmmm," she said thoughtfully. "Hmmm."

Finally, she spoke.

"Child," said Grandmother Willow, "it seems to me this spinning arrow is pointing you down your path."

"I know," said Pocahontas. "But what *is* my path? How am I ever going to find it?"

Grandmother Willow chuckled softly to herself.

"Your mother asked me the very same question."

"What did you tell her?" asked Pocahontas.

"I told her to listen. All around you are spirits, Child. They live in the Earth, the Water, the Sky. Listen to them. If you listen, they will guide you."

A light breeze rustled through Grandmother Willow's leaves.

"I can hear the wind," said Pocahontas.

"What is it telling you?" asked Grandmother Willow.

Pocahontas listened quietly. Then she sighed. "I don't know."

"There is more than listening with your ears," said Grandmother Willow. "You must listen with your heart. *Then* you will understand."

Pocahontas closed her eyes and listened again.

After a minute or two, her eyes flew open.

"The wind is saying something!" she cried. "It says something's coming." Then she looked confused. "*Strange clouds?*"

Pocahontas looked puzzled.

"What is it?" asked Grandmother Willow.

"The wind is telling me to climb to the top of *you!*" she told her.

"Well," said Grandmother Willow, "better get going!"

Pulling herself up from limb to limb, Pocahontas climbed to the top.

"What do you see?" asked Grandmother Willow.

"Clouds!" answered Pocahontas.

She sucked in her breath. "*Strange clouds.*"

In the distance, the huge white sails of the *Susan Constant* billowed above the treetops.

Aboard the *Susan Constant*, Governor Ratcliffe flung open the porthole. He gaped at the forest that lined the coast.

"Look at it, Wiggins," he said. "An entire New World chock full of gold. Just waiting for me."

Wiggins was serving Percy his dinner. The pudgy dog sniffed the steaming food. After he inspected it, he held up his jowly chin.

"We'll have scores of adventures, too. Won't we,

Percy!" Wiggins said, as he tied a napkin around the dog's neck.

Percy ignored him and nibbled his dinner.

"Do you think we'll meet some Indians?" Wiggins asked the governor.

"If we do," said Ratcliffe, "we shall be sure to give them a proper greeting."

"Bang, Bang," said Wiggins, picking up a large spoon and pointing it like a gun. "I do love a fracas!"

John Smith poked his head through the cabin door.

"This is a perfect place to anchor, Governor!" he exclaimed. "The water's deep enough. We can pull up close to shore."

"Well then, give the order for the landing boats," said Ratcliffe. "Oh, about the natives. I'm counting on you to make sure they don't disrupt our mission."

"Don't worry, Sir," said John. "If they're anything like the ones I've fought before, it's nothing I can't handle." He smiled, gave a quick salute, and left.

Governor Ratcliffe frowned. "The men like Smith, don't they?" he said to Wiggins.

"Don't worry, Sir," said Wiggins. "Once they get to know you, I'm sure they'll like you, too."

"Well, I don't give a hoot if they like me or not!" said Ratcliffe. "When King James sees all the gold I bring back, success will be mine, at last!"

John Smith climbed from a rowing boat on to the

pebbly beach. He stared up at the forest of towering trees. They were the tallest trees he'd ever seen!

"I've never seen anything like it!" said Thomas. "And to think – it's all ours!"

John strode across the shore and pulled himself up into a tall pine.

"John," Thomas called up to him. "What are you doing?"

"Getting a better look," John answered, climbing higher and higher. He gazed at the river and land that spread out beneath him.

Not far away, Pocahontas was also trying to get a better look. Hiding behind a bush on a rocky ledge, she watched him climb the tree.

Meeko leaned out over the ledge.

"Shh," Pocahontas whispered, trying to hold onto him. The man was was climbing right towards them! Meeko wiggled out of her grasp.

John stopped climbing. What was that rustling sound on the cliff? He grabbed his knife from his boot.

Pocahontas held her breath.

"Will you look at this!" John said to himself, sticking his knife back into his boot. He reached out and picked up the curious raccoon. "You're a strange-looking fellow."

Meeko sniffed at the leather pouch tied to John's belt.

John reached inside and pulled out a biscuit.

"You hungry?" he asked. "Here you go. It's a biscuit. It's food. Well, sort of."

Meeko grabbed the biscuit and gobbled it right down.

"You like it, eh?" asked John. "But just try eating it for four months straight."

Pocahontas smiled with relief. The man was not going to hurt Meeko. In fact, he seemed kind. Pocahontas leaned further out for a better look.

Meeko picked some crumbs from the ground. After he ate them he looked towards Pocahontas.

John glanced over at the ledge. "You've got a friend back there?" he asked.

Pocahontas held her breath and leaned back as far as she could. The man was practically staring her in the face!

Humming frantically, Flit burst out of the shadows and dived at John's head.

John threw up his arm to protect himself. Again and again Flit whirled straight at him. Then Thomas called from the beach.

"John, you'd better get down here. The Governor's coming ashore!"

"All right, all right," John said to Flit. "I'm leaving."

As he climbed down the tree, Pocahontas blew out her breath. That was too close!

She stared down at the *Susan Constant*. She couldn't wait to tell Nakoma about her adventure – and the strange-looking man who liked to climb trees!

The Village Council called a hasty meeting.

"I saw them from the ridge," said one warrior. "They're starting to come ashore! They have hair on their faces – like dogs! And did you see their skin? It's pale and sickly."

Another warrior spoke up. "I have never seen such a boat. It must come from the Great Waters."

Chief Powhatan raised his hand and the room fell silent.

"My brothers," he said, "we must know more about these visitors."

He turned to the village medicine man. "Kekata," he asked, "what do you see?"

Kekata poured a handful of powder on the fire. A plume of smoke rose from the flames. As it changed shape, he studied it.

"These are not men like us," he said. "They prowl the earth like wolves, consuming everything in their path. And their weapons spout fire and thunder!"

Kocoum rose to his feet. "Great Powhatan," he said, "I will lead our warriors to the river and attack. We will destroy these invaders!"

Noisily, the rest of the warriors agreed.

"Kocoum," said Powhatan, speaking firmly. "In past battles, we knew our enemy. But these pale visitors are strange to us. Take some men to the river to observe them."

Then he spoke to the assembled villagers. "Let us hope they do not intend to stay."

Down at the beach, another meeting was being held. Governor Ratcliffe stood several yards back from the shore. He clutched a British flag high in one hand. Then he spoke loudly.

"I hearby claim this land and all its riches in the name of His Majesty, King James, and do so name this settlement . . . Jamestown!"

He jammed the flag pole into the ground.

"Well, Smith," he said turning to John, "it appears I've selected the perfect location. Not a native in sight."

"Sir," answered John, "just because we don't see them doesn't mean they're not out there."

"Perhaps, then," suggested Ratcliffe, "you should venture forth and determine their whereabouts?"

"Yes, Sir," said John, grabbing his musket. "If there are any Indians out there, I'll find them!"

23

"Fine," said Ratcliffe. "And while you're gone, the rest of the men will break out the shovels and start digging. Let's not forget what the Spanish found when they came to the New World. GOLD! Mountains of it!"

As he headed into the forest, John could hear the men singing loudly as they dug for gold.

Later that day, deep in the woods, John stopped at the edge of a waterfall. He cupped his hands in the icy water. But as he leaned forward to drink, a reflection caught his eye. Someone was behind him!

John spun round. He was all alone. But he trusted instincts; someone was definitely watching him. He leapt across the stream and disappeared behind the water fall where he waited. Then, with his musket ready to fire, he leapt out onto a rock and took steady aim – and hardly believed what he saw. It was a young woman! She had dark eyes and her long black hair shone in the dappled light. She was the most beautiful woman he had ever seen! He instantly lowered his musket.

Pocahontas stood, equally shocked and still, except for the wind that blew her hair across her face and neck. She was staring back at the man who'd been in the tree. The man with yellow hair that glinted like sunlight, and eyes as blue as a robin's egg.

Slowly, John Smith removed his helmet and stepped towards Pocahontas.

"It's all right," he said. "I'm not going to hurt you."

But his movement and voice were enough to break the trance that had held Pocahontas there. She quickly turned and ran.

"No, wait, please," he called after her. "Don't run off."

Pocahontas ran to the riverbank, thankful that her canoe was in sight. She stepped in and was about to push off, when she heard Smith's voice again. Pocahontas hesitated a moment and looked back. The man's voice was kind. And after all, he'd been very nice to Meeko.

John caught her up and offered her his hand.

"Here," he said, "let me help you out of there."

Pocahontas stood facing him.

"Who are you?" John whispered.

"*Mat-ta-que-nat-o-rath*. I do not understand," said Pocahontas.

"How foolish of me," John thought. "She doesn't understand what I'm saying!"

A slight breeze sprang up and swirled about them. Pocahontas caught her breath. The wind was speaking to her. It was carrying Grandmother Willow's words!

> *Listen with your heart,*
> *Then you will understand.*

Pocahontas pointed to herself.

"Pocahontas," she said to the man. "My name is Pocahontas."

John smiled. So she *did* understand him.

"My name is John Smith," he said, pointing to himself.

Pocahontas took John's outstretched hand and together they walked through the forest.

5

At the edge of a clearing, hidden behind a gooseberry bush, Kocoum spied on the white men. His comrade, Namontack, silently crept up behind him.

"There are thirty more down by the ridge," he whispered.

"That makes more than a hundred," said Kocoum. "Look at them. First they cut down the trees. Then they push sticks deep into the ground! What do they wish to find?"

As he spoke, there was a loud CRACK in the distance. Then the ground shuddered beneath their feet.

Namontack's eyes shone with anger.

"Another tree has fallen," he said.

"I wish we knew what they were saying," said Kocoum. "That fat one over there – the one eating – I think he is their chief."

*

Governor Ratcliffe, holding a greasy plate, gnawed noisily on a chicken leg.

"That's it, that's it, keep at it, men!" he called out. "Keep digging. The gold's got to be here somewhere!"

He looked at the pile of bones on his plate.

"Where's Wiggins?" he roared.

"Right here, Sir," answered Wiggins, appearing instantly at his side.

"Dispose of this!" Ratcliffe ordered, handing him the plate.

"Perhaps Percy would like to nibble on one of the bones," suggested Wiggins.

"Fetch!" he told the little dog, throwing a bone into a gooseberry bush at the edge of the clearing.

Percy scrambled after the bone – and tore straight into Namontack and Kocoum! Startled, he yelped and leaped high into the air. The warriors, equally surprised, jumped to their feet.

"What's happened to my poor Percy," Ratcliffe shouted. Then he saw Kocoum and Namontack.

"IT'S AN AMBUSH!" he screamed. "Men, arm yourselves!"

Thomas and the others quickly scrambled to find their muskets.

"Where's Smith when I need him," Ratcliffe cried, grabbing a musket. He took aim, and fired.

The blast caught Namontack's leg. Clutching

his wound, the warrior fell to the ground.

"Namontack!" cried Kocoum. He raced to help his friend.

One of the settlers sprang from the bushes, ready to club Kocoum with the butt of his rifle.

Kocoum wrestled him to the ground. He struck at the man's chest with his stone knife, but the knife blade simply snapped off. He saw that the man's chest was protected by a shiny hard plate.

As more white men headed towards him, Kocoum was overcome by a fear he had never known. For the first time, he felt defenseless. Terrible thoughts flew through his head: how could his people fight these pale strangers? These men wore clothing that shattered stone. And Kekata was right – their weapons exploded like thunder and lightning!

Horrified, Kocoum knew that he could do nothing but flee. He hoisted his injured friend over his shoulder and retreated.

Chief Powhatan knelt beside Namontack as Kekata tended the terrible wound. The medicine man sadly shook his head.

"This is a wound is strange to me," he said.

Rage boiled within Powhatan.

"They invade our shore, destroy our land," he said. He stared at the wounded man. "And now this!"

He rose and spoke with Kocoum.

"We will fight this enemy," he said. "Send messengers to every village in our nation. We will call on our brothers to help us."

Then Powhatan addressed the villagers.

"*No one* is to go near the white men," he ordered. "These creatures, who come from the Never-Ending Waters – they are savages!"

Pocahontas sat at the edge of the river, studying John Smith's helmet.

Sitting down on the grass beside her, John asked, "Where do you live?"

"My village is on the Chicahominy," Pocahontas answered.

"Chica-hominy?" asked John.

"It's a river," explained Pocahontas. "It flows into this river – the Quiyoughcohannock."

John shook his head in wonder. "You have the most unusual names here . . . Chicahominy . . . Quiyoughcohannock . . . Pocahontas."

"Your name is unusual, too," Pocahontas told him. "*John Smith*. What does it mean?"

"It's just a name."

Pocahontas was surprised. "How strange. All our names mean something."

"And what does *Pocahontas* mean?" John asked her.

Pocahontas grinned. "*Little Mischief,*" she said.

She patted Meeko, who had just waddled up from the brook. "And this is Meeko."

John hid his surprise. This looked like the same animal he'd given the biscuit to.

He held out his hand. "How do you do, Meeko?" he asked.

Pocahontas looked confused.

"It's all right," explained John. "It's just a handshake. Let me show you."

He shook Pocahontas's hand. "It's how we say hello."

Pocahontas smiled. "This is how *we* say hello." She held her hand up, palm facing outwards and moved it in a circle in the air.

"*Wing-gap-o,*" she said.

John copied her. "*Wing-gap-o.*"

Then Pocahontas moved her hand in a circle back the other way. "And this is how we say goodbye."

John grinned and put his hand up against hers. "I'd rather we stay with hello!"

Buzzing importantly, Flit landed on Pocahontas' shoulder and shook his bill at John.

"Flit doesn't like strangers," Pocahontas explained.

John held out his finger and tried to coax Flit to hop onto it.

"But I'm not a stranger any more, am I, Flit?" he

asked the tiny hummingbird.

Flit turned his bill away.

John laughed. "Stubborn little fellow, isn't he?"

Pocahontas nodded and smiled. "Very stubborn."

Meeko began to sniff the air.

"Here," said John. He untied the leather pouch that hung from his belt and took out a biscuit. "I know what he" – Meeko snatched the biscuit and gobbled it down. – "wants," finished John.

Hunting for more food, Meeko grabbed the pouch and poked his head inside. But instead of finding another biscuit, he reappeared with a compass clenched between his teeth. Growling with delight, he carried it up the nearest tree.

"Meeko, come back with that," scolded Pocahontas. "It doesn't belong to you!"

"Oh, it's all right," said John. "He can keep it."

"What was it?" Pocahontas asked.

"Just my compass," said John.

"Compass?" asked Pocahontas.

"It tells you how to find your way when you get lost," John explained to her. "But it's all right. I can always buy another one when I get back to London."

"London?" asked Pocahontas. "Is that your village?"

"Yes," said John. "A very *big* village."

"What is it like?"

"Oh," said John, "it has streets filled with

carriages, bridges over the rivers, buildings as tall as trees . . ."

Pocahontas' eyes grew round. "I'd like to see those things."

John smiled at her. "You will."

"How?" asked Pocahontas, very surprised.

"We're going to build them here," said John. "We'll show your people how to use this land properly. How to make the most of it."

"Make the most of it?" asked Pocahontas.

"Yes," said John. "We'll build roads and decent houses . . ."

Pocahontas got to her feet.

"Our houses are fine," she said. With that, she walked down the bank and climbed back into the canoe.

"Wait a minute," said John, holding the canoe.

"Let go," said Pocahontas.

"You think your houses are fine only because you don't know any better!" John went on. "There's so much we can teach you. We've improved the lives of savages all over the world."

Pocahontas was stunned. "*Savages*?!"

John tried to explain. "It's just a word. You know, a term for people who are uncivilized."

"Like me?" asked Pocahontas, not hiding her anger.

"Well," stumbled John. "When I say uncivilized,

what I mean is . . ."

Pocahontas climbed out of the canoe and finished the sentence for him. "What you mean is," she said poking him in the chest, "not like *you*!" She looked hard into John's eyes. "You think your people know everything. But my people know this land as yours never will."

John followed her into the forest. "The creatures of the forest, each rock and every bird, the fish in the waters – they are our Brothers and Sisters. We all live together. We are all one – with the Sun, the Moon and the Stars."

John Smith listened to what she had to say. He followed her further into the forest, more and more drawn by her words. After a while, they rested by a little stream. A leaf drifted down and landed in the water. Pocahontas handed it to John.

"Even this little leaf has a spirit and a name."

John smiled sceptically.

"Do you not see?" she continued. "You, me, Meeko and Flit, the rainstorms and mountaintops – we are all a part of the Earth. We are joined to each other."

She formed a circle with her arms. "My people say life on Earth is like a giant hoop. It has no beginning. And it has no end.

I think your people do not understand the Earth. They think it is a dead thing.

As Pocahontas spoke, John felt a change come over him. He had never seen someone so at home in her world. What she was saying to made sense. He looked at her with a new understanding.

Pocahontas no longer felt angry. The two gazed into each other's eyes for what seemed like a long time.

But then Pocahontas suddenly looked away.

"What is it?" John asked.

"The drums," said Pocahontas. "They mean trouble. Something is happening in the village. I have to go."

John pulled her close. "Will I see you again?"

Pocahontas had never felt so confused. Here was a man who had insulted her people – and yet, she liked him – very much!

"I shouldn't be here," she said.

"I want to see you again," said John.

"I have to go," Pocahontas whispered.

Feeling both happy and sad, she ran home.

The next morning was rainy. John watched in silence as Lon and Ben raised another section of the fort wall.

Thomas appeared lugging a thick plank. "Think this'll keep the natives out?" he asked. "This stockade'll close in the whole settlement."

John didn't answer as he stared up at the wall.

"Something wrong, John?" asked Thomas. "You've been awfully quiet lately."

"Aw," said Ben, "he's just sad he wasn't there the other day when the Indians attacked us! But don't worry, mate. You'll get your chance!"

"Right," said Thomas, "If any Indians show up, John'll take care of them!"

Inside his luxurious tent, Governor Ratcliffe paced back and forth, wringing his hands with worry.

"Wiggins," he complained, "we should be

wallowing in riches by now. Why can't we find gold? What am I overlooking?"

There was no answer.

"Wiggins?" asked Ratcliffe, glancing around.

At that moment, Wiggins came stumbling in the doorway.

"This is it, Governor, I'm done for," he moaned and fell to the ground. An arrow was sticking out of his chest.

"INDIANS!" shrieked Ratcliffe.

Wiggins laughed and hopped to his feet. "Just kidding," he said. He pulled the fake arrow off of his head. "See? I made it myself!"

Ratcliffe snatched away the arrow.

"You idiot," he said. Then his mouth dropped open.

"That's it!" cried Ratcliffe, waving his arms. "It's the *Indians*! *They* have the gold. They have it and they don't want us to take it from them."

"Well, we'll just have to take it by force, won't we," said Ratcliffe, rubbing his hands together.

He dashed outside. "You there," he called out to Thomas, "where's Captain Smith?"

Thomas glanced round. John was gone. "He was just here, sir," he said. "Maybe he went off into the woods."

Ratcliffe pointed to Lon and Ben. "Well then, you there, go and find him!" he shouted.

Lon gulped. "What if we run into Indians?" he asked.

Ratcliffe glared at him. How stupid the man was!

"That's what guns are for," he told him. "Now arm yourselves and get moving!"

Just then Meeko, tore out of the Governor's tent. Percy dashed out behind, barking furiously, across the settlement and ran straight between Ratcliffe's legs.

"I say, what's going on here!" demanded Ratcliffe.

Wiggins appeared next waving his arms.

"That thieving black-eyed beast sneaked in and snatched some of Percy's food," he said between gasps. "And now, I'm afraid, Sir, your little doggie has disappeared into the woods!"

On the other side of the forest, the warriors were building their own wall. They'd worked all night in the rain. By morning, a stout palisade of tall poles surrounded the village.

Pocahontas and Nakoma were out in the wet field picking corn.

Nakoma stopped to rest. She wiped bits of damp corn silk from her deerskin dress.

"I'm glad the rain's stopped," she said. "But I'll be really happy when the walls are finished. I didn't sleep at all last night."

"Pocahontas," a voice called. Pocahontas turned. It was her father.

"You and Nakoma should be inside the village," Powhatan told her.

"We won't be long, Father," said Pocahontas.

"We're gathering more food. It will be needed when the warriors arrive," explained Nakoma.

Powhatan smiled. "That is true. But don't go far. Now is not the time to be running off."

"Yes, Father," said Pocahontas.

He looked at the necklace he had given her.

"When I see you wear that necklace, Pocahontas," he said, "you look just like your mother."

Pocahontas fingered the white shell. "I miss her," she said, softly. "I wish she was here."

A little breeze sprang up and rustled the corns stalks.

"She is," said Powhatan, gazing at the forest. "Whenever the wind moves in the trees, I feel her presence."

He smiled at Pocahontas. "I will tell Kocoum that you are out in the cornfield," he said. "He can watch over you."

As soon as he left, Nakoma spoke.

"Pocahontas, I know you so well," she said. "You're hiding something. What is it?"

"I'm not hiding anything . . ." said Pocahontas.

"Yes, you are," said Nakoma. "You can tell me, I promise I won't tell any—"

Then she gasped. A white man, crouching low, was

40

coming out of the woods. He was coming straight towards *them*!

"What is it?" asked Pocahontas, looking round. Her heart thumped. It was John Smith!

Nakoma started to yell for help, but Pocahontas quickly covered her friend's mouth. "It's all right," she said.

Shocked, Nakoma saw Pocahontas speaking to the stranger.

"What are you doing here?" Pocahontas whispered.

"I wanted to see you again," John whispered back. "I didn't have a chance to say goodbye."

A man shouted from across the field. "Pocahontas!" It was Kocoum! He was heading towards them.

Pocahontas squeezed Nakoma's arm.

"Please don't say anything," she pleaded. Pocahontas grabbed John's hand and while Nakoma watched in disbelief, two fled through the rows of tall corn.

A few moments later, Nakoma greeted Kocoum.

"Where is Pocahontas?" he asked.

"Pocahontas?" asked Nakoma. "Let me think. Hmm. I don't think I've seen her."

Kocoum gestured towards the village. "But Powhatan just said she was with you."

"Oh, well, yes," stammered Nakoma. "She was.

But now she . . . isn't.''

Kocoum looked suspicious. Then he spoke in an unusually gentle voice.

"Pocahontas can't keep running off," he said. It's dangerous out there. Nakoma, you must tell her that. She listens to you.''

As Kocoum walked away, Nakoma looked back at the forest. If Kocoum only knew!

Pocahontas led John further away from the village.

"I can't believe you came to the village," she said. "If any of the warriors had seen you . . .''

"Where are we going?" he asked.

"To a place where nobody will find us. It's my favourite place," said Pocahontas.

They followed a winding stream that flowed into the heart of the forest. Then they stepped out into a sunny glade. In the wooded shadows, a doe and her fawn drank quietly at the stream. Beside the water stood an enormous willow. John followed Pocahontas up onto a large stump in front of the tree. Meeko climbed up behind them.

"One look at this beautiful place," he said, "and the men will forget all about digging for gold.''

"Gold?" Pocahontas asked.

"Yes," said John, "that's why we're here.''

"What's gold?''

John stopped to think. "Well," he tried to explain,

Above: Pocahontas, the beautiful daughter of Chief Powhatan, makes her way through the peaceful forest surrounding her village. Meeko the racoon tags along.

Below: After a long voyage, the *Susan Constant* arrives in Virginia. The Englishmen aboard hope to find gold in the New World.

Above: Pocahontas is intrigued by the strange visitors who have come ashore.

Below: Ratcliffe, the greedy governor of the New World expedition, orders his men to dig for gold.

Above: Captain John Smith scouts the terrain for natives.

Below: Fascinated by the blond-haired, blue-eyed stranger, Pocahontas secretly follows Smith.

Above: John Smith senses that he is being followed.

Below: As Smith takes aim with his musket, he is shocked to discover Pocahontas, the most beautiful woman he has ever seen.

Above: Despite their cultural differences, Pocahontas and John Smith fall in love.

Below: Pocahontas teaches Smith that he must respect the earth and all its creatures.

Above: Provoked by Ratcliffe and the settlers, Powhatan's
warriors prepare to attack.

Below: After seeing her best friend with John Smith, Nakoma
worries that Pocahontas is in danger.

Above: As tension mounts between the settlers and the
Powhatan people, Thomas searches for John Smith,
who has mysteriously disappeared.

Below: Blamed for Kocoum's death, Smith is captured by
Powhatan's warriors and sentenced to death.

Above: Pocahontas sneaks in to see John Smith one last time.

Below: Powhatan raises his club, preparing to kill Smith.
Within seconds, Pocahontas will save Smith's life.

"it's yellow and comes out of the ground. It is *very* valuable."

Pocahontas reached into the woven bag that hung from her shoulder. She pulled out an ear of freshly-picked corn. Yanking back the husk, she pointed to the rows of shiny yellow kernels. "Here," she said, handing it to him. "We have lots of gold."

John smiled and tasted it.

"This is very good," he said, putting the corn into his pouch. "But it is not gold." He took a coin from his pocket. *This* is gold."

Pocahontas studied the strange object in his hand. Meeko took the coin out of Smith's hand and bit it. Disappointed, he tossed it back and scrambled high up into the tree's branches. "There is nothing like that round here."

"Are you sure?" asked John.

Pocahontas nodded. "Not that I have ever seen."

"Well," said John, mostly to himself, "the men aren't going to like this."

Pocahontas looked relieved. "Does this mean they'll leave?"

John shrugged his shoulders. "I don't know. Some might."

"But what about you?" she asked. "Will you go back home – to London?"

"I don't know," answered John. "It's not like I have much of a home to go back to. I suppose I've never really belonged anywhere."

"You could belong here," Pocahontas said softly.

John gazed high into the sweeping branches, as a gentle wind rustled through the leaves. Then he gasped. Just for a moment, an old woman's face had appeared on the side of the tree! Amazed and scared, he sprang to his feet.

"What was that!" he asked.

Pocahontas tried not to smile. "Did you see something?"

John shook his head. "No, no. I just . . . uh . . . I didn't see anything – did I?"

"Look again," Pocahontas told him.

John stared at the tree. Slowly, before his eyes, the old woman's face appeared again!

"Hello, John Smith," she said.

John was almost struck speechless. "Pocahontas," he whispered, ". . . that tree . . . it's . . . it's talking to me."

"Then you should talk back," Pocahontas whispered.

"Don't be frightened, young man," said Grandmother Willow. "My bark is worse than my bite."

John couldn't believe it. The tree was making jokes!

"Say something," Pocahontas urged him.

"What do you say to a *tree*?" John asked under his breath.

Pocahontas smiled. "Anything you like."

John took a step forward and took a deep breath. "So, you, uh . . . live here," he stammered.

Grandmother Willow chuckled. "Come closer, John Smith."

John took another step.

Grandmother Willow took a long look at him.

"He has a good soul," she said to Pocahontas. "And he's handsome, too."

John grinned and turned to Pocahontas. "I like her."

Pocahontas grinned back. "I knew you would."

"Smith! Smith!" shouted a man's voice. "Where are you, mate? Ratcliffe's looking for ya!"

"It's my men," said John. "We can't let them see us!"

"Quickly," said Grandmother Willow. "Hide behind me!"

In a few minutes, Ben and Lon broke through the underbush.

Lon glanced nervously about the open sunny glade.

"This place gives me the creeps," he said. "Indians could be hiding here."

"Well, if you spot one," said Ben, "don't ask questions – just shoot!"

He looked up at Grandmother Willow. "Lon! Will you look at the size of this tree!"

As they stepped forward for a closer look, Ben suddenly tripped.

"Watch your feet, you big oaf," he snapped at Lon.

Lon had turned pale. "It wasn't me!" he gasped. "It was the tree. I saw it. That root just rose out of the ground – and tripped you!"

"Have you gone mad, mate?" asked Ben. "How could a root just . . ."

He kicked it with his boot. Before his eyes, the root slid back underground.

"Let's get out of here!" yelled Ben.

"What about Smith?" Lon asked, panting after him.

"He's a big lad," answered Ben. "He can take care of himself!"

John and Pocahontas stepped out from behind Grandmother Willow.

"I'd better get back," said John, "before they send the whole camp after me."

"When will I see you again?" asked Pocahontas.

"Meet me tonight," he said. "Right here."

Pocahontas nodded.

"When the moon rises," she said, softly.

"I'll be waiting."

"Grandmother Willow," Pocahontas asked after he was gone, "what am I doing? I shouldn't see him again. But I *want* to see him again."

"Who wouldn't?" asked Grandmother Willow. "*I* want to see him again too!"

"I'm supposed to stay in the village," said Pocahontas, "but still, something inside is telling me it's the right thing."

Grandmother Willow thought for a minute. "Perhaps it's your dream," she suggested.

"My dream . . ." said Pocahontas. "Grandmother Willow! Maybe he's the one the spinning arrow was pointing to!"

Grandmother Willow smiled. "It appears, my dear, that you have found your path. You must listen with your heart."

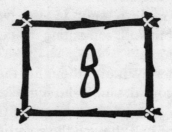

8

Pocahontas hurried home. When she ran into the village she heard shouts and loud cheers coming from the river. She joined the excited crowd to see what was going on.

Warriors with painted faces, ready for battle, were paddling their long canoes towards shore. As they beached their boats, the villagers swarmed around to greet them.

Pocahontas felt someone touch her on the shoulder. It was Kocoum.

"Kocoum!" cried Pocahantas. "What is happening?"

His eyes gleamed bright. "Look at them!" he said. "Our brothers have joined with us. Now we have enough warriors to destroy those demons!

"I must go now," he said. "The war council is gathering for a meeting."

Pocahontas frantically searched the crowd for her

father. She caught up with him before he entered the meeting.

"Father," she pleaded, "I need to speak with you."

"Not now, my daughter," said Powhatan. "The War Council is gathering."

Pocahontas blocked his way. Powhatan stopped in surprise.

"We don't have to fight them!" she said. "There must be a better path."

Her father looked stern. "Sometimes our paths are chosen for us."

Pocahontas tried to think fast. "But perhaps . . . perhaps we should try talking to them?"

Powhatan frowned. "They do not want to talk."

He started to go.

Pocahontas grabbed his arm. "But what if one of them *did* want to talk?" she asked. "You would listen to him, wouldn't you, Father?"

"Pocahontas," Powhatan began, impatiently.

"*Wouldn't you?*" she persisted.

"Of course I would," he said.

Pocahontas sighed with relief.

"But it is not that simple," Powhatan added. "Nothing is simple any more."

He touched Pocahontas lightly on her cheek.

"This is a very dangerous time, my Daughter," he told her. "Please stay here where it is safe."

Then he went inside to begin the War Council.

At the entrance gate at Jamestown, Thomas stood on sentry duty. When he heard a branch snap in the woods, he whirled round and aimed his musket.

"Easy, Thomas!" John called out. "It's just me!"

"John," said Thomas. His voice shook. "I could have killed you!"

"Not aiming like that you couldn't," said John.

He took the musket, raised it to his own shoulder and aimed.

"Keep both eyes open like this when you shoot," he instructed Thomas. "You'll see twice as well."

Ben and Lon ran up to them. "Smith, there you are! We were looking all over for you."

Before John could speak, Governor Ratcliffe stormed over to him.

"SMITH!" he shouted. "Where have you been?"

"Scouting the terrain, sir," John answered him.

Ratcliffe beamed. "Excellent! Then you must know the Indians' whereabouts. We'll need that information for the battle."

"What battle?" asked John.

"We are going to eliminate the Indians once and for all!" Ratcliffe told him.

John was stunned. "No, you can't do that!"

Ratcliffe narrowed his eyes. "Oh, can't I?"

"Look," said John, "we don't have to fight them."

50

Thomas's jaw dropped. "John, what's happened to you?"

"I met one of them," said John.

"You met a savage?!" asked Thomas.

"They're not savages!" John said. "They can help us. They know the land, how to navigate the rivers . . ."

He pulled the ear of corn out of his leather pouch.

"And look at this!" he said. "They have food!"

Governor Ratcliffe grabbed it from him.

"They don't want to feed us, they want to kill us," he shouted. "They've got our gold and they're trying to keep it from us!"

"But there *is* no gold!" John explained.

"No gold?" said Ben. "Then why are we here?"

"I suppose your new Indian friend told you this?" asked Ratcliffe, suspiciously.

John nodded.

"Lies! Lies!" yelled Ratcliffe. "There's no room for them in a civilized society . . ."

"But this is their land!" John broke in.

Ratcliffe shook his fist. "This is *my* land!" he shouted. *I* make the laws here!"

He stopped to think for a moment. Then he roared, "And I say this – anyone who sees an Indian must kill him!"

He leaned close to John's face. "Any man who

51

disobeys my orders will be tried for treason and hanged.''

Pocahontas watched the sun sink behind the trees. Soon the moon would rise! Looking around hurriedly, she searched for a break in the palisade wall.

Someone stepped out of the shadows. It was Nakoma. "I know what you're doing," she said. "Don't go!"

Pocahontas nervously raised a finger to her lips. "Shh!" she said, "I won't be gone long."

"I lied for you once," said Nakoma. "Don't ask me to do it again. Pocahontas, he is one of them. He's a killer!"

"You don't know him," said Pocahontas.

"How can *you* know him?" asked Nakoma. "You don't even speak his language!"

Pocahontas smiled. "We speak with our hearts," she said.

"Do not say such foolish things!" Nakoma told her. "Pocahontas, if you go out there, you'll be turning your back on your own people."

Pocahontas looked intently at her friend. "I'm trying to help my people."

Nakoma sighed. It was no use.

"Pocahontas," she said softly, "you're my friend. I don't want you to get hurt."

"I won't," said Pocahontas. "I know what I am doing."

She squeezed into a narrow opening.

"Pocahontas, no!" said Nakoma. She tried to grab her arm, but Pocahontas had already slipped away into the darkening forest.

Nakoma didn't know what to do. If she did nothing, Pocahontas might be captured, or even killed! But how could she betray her dearest friend?

Then she made up her mind. It was more important for Pocahontas to be safe! She decided to tell Kocoum.

She hurried back through the village. Kocoum was outside his hut sharpening a stone knife blade. He looked up at Nakoma.

"Kocoum," she said, hesitantly. "I have something to tell you about Pocahontas. I think . . . she's in trouble."

As the moon rose in the sky, she told him what had happened.

Thomas stood quietly in the shadows and watched John disappear into the forest. Then he felt a heavy hand on his shoulder. Startled, he spun round and found himself face to face with Governor Ratcliffe.

"Follow him," said Ratcliffe. "I want to know where he's sneaking off to."

"Yes, Sir," said Thomas.

"And, remember," snarled Ratcliffe. "If you happen to see any Indians – shoot them! You've been a slipshod sailor and a poor excuse for a soldier, Ratcliffe continued. "Don't disappoint me again!"

Pocahontas ran into the moonlit glade.

"What's happening, Child?"asked Grandmother Willow. "I feel the Earth is trembling with fear."

At that moment John came into sight.

As soon as Pocahontas saw him, she flew into his arms.

"Pocahontas," he said, "listen to me. We don't have much time! My men are planning to attack your village. You've got to warn them."

Pocahontas was stunned by the news. "Our village is filled with warriors. They are planning to attack *your* people!"

She took John's hand and began to pull him. "Before it's too late," she said, "you have to come with me and talk to my father."

"Your father?" asked John.

Pocahontas nodded. "He said he'd talk to anyone who comes in peace."

"It's not that easy," John told her. "I don't think talking is going to do any good."

"But we have to do *something*!" said Pocahontas.

John sadly shook his head. "I already tried talking to my men. It's no use."

Pocahontas suddenly turned at the sound of muffled howl coming from the woods.

Meeko and Flit appeared from the underbrush. And staggering behind was Percy, his head stuck in a small log. Exhausted, the little dog fell in a heap.

"That's the strangest creature I've ever seen," remarked Grandmother Willow.

"Percy!" said John, freeing him from the log. "Are you all right?"

As soon as Percy was unstuck, he scrambled to his feet, growled, and sprang after Meeko. Wildly, the animals chased each other round and round Grandmother Willow.

"Meeko!" scolded Pocahontas. "Stop it! What are you doing?"

John made a lunge at Percy, finally chasing him onto Grandmother Willow's stump.

"You see what I mean?" said John. "We can't even stop two little animals from fighting. How do you expect us to stop two armies?"

Grandmother Willow spoke up. "I can't believe I'm hearing this!"

John and Pocahontas looked up in surprise.

"Come over here," said Grandmother Willow. She reached down and dipped one of her branches into the water. "Look!"

John peered into the moonlit stream. "I can't see anything."

"The ripples . . ." said Pocahontas looking closely.

"Yes," said Grandmother Willow. "So small at first, then look how they grow.

"But," she added, nudging John with a branch, "someone has to start them."

John leaned over. For several moments, he studied the widening rings of water.

"And that someone is us?" John said, looking up at Grandmother Willow.

"Pocahontas," he said standing up straight. "Let's go and talk to your father."

Pocahontas threw her arms round his neck and kissed him.

Suddenly, Kocoum, shrieking a fierce war cry, crashed through the glade and sprang at John. Caught off balance, John fell to the ground. Pocahontas screamed as Kocoum pulled out his knife.

John grabbed the furious warrior's hand and shoved him away. But Kocoum lunged at John again.

"Kocoum, no!" screamed Pocahontas.

At that moment Thomas tore into the glade. Seeing the fight, he raised his musket, closed one eye and took careful aim.

"Both eyes open," he reminded himself. He opened both eyes. Then he fired.

Kocoum clutched his chest and sank to his knees.

John spun around. "Thomas!" he gasped.

Pocahontas flew to Kocoum's side and tried to support him.

As Kocoum slipped to the ground, his hand caught in Pocahontas' necklace. The string broke and the necklace fell.

"You killed him!" Pocahontas screamed at Thomas. "You killed Kocoum!"

Thomas started to move towards Kocoum. "I didn't mean . . . He was trying . . . I thought that . . ."

Pocahontas flew at Thomas. "Get away from him!"

"He was only trying to protect me," John said, trying to hold her back.

"He killed him!" sobbed Pocahontas.

Then the sound of war cries filled the forest. They were growing louder and louder.

"Thomas," ordered John, "get out of here!"

Thomas, pale with shock, stared at Kocoum's lifeless body.

"GET OUT OF HERE!" John roared at him.

His eyes stinging with tears, Thomas bolted into the thicket.

Moments later, the moonlit glade swarmed with warriors. Seeing Kocoum's body their eyes filled with fury. Four of them seized John, tied his hands, and dragged him away.

The other warriors gently lifted up Kocoum's body. Hoisting it high above their shoulders, they carried their dead comrade back home.

Grief-stricken, Pocahontas rose and slowly walked back home. Side by side, Meeko and Percy followed sadly behind.

Chief Powhatan felt his heart break. He stood under the stars as the warriors placed Kocoum's body at his feet. His face looked hard as stone.

"Who did this?" he demanded.

The warriors shoved John forward.

"My Chief," one of them said, "Pocahontas was out in the woods. Kocoum went to find her. This white man attacked them."

Powhatan looked straight into John's eyes.

"Your weapons are strong," he told him. "But now my anger is stronger."

Then, in the fading moonlight, he addressed the grieving villagers.

"At sunrise," he roared, "he will be the first to die."

As the warriors started to drag John away, Pocahontas flew up to her father.

"Father, wait!" she cried.

Powhatan spun round and took her aside.

"Pocahontas," he said. "I told you to stay in the village. You disobeyed me! You have shamed your father!"

"But Father," Pocahontas tried to explain, "I was only trying to help."

"Because of your foolishness," said Powhatan, "Kocoum is dead."

Pocahontas felt crushed by his words. What he said was awful and true. She knew he would hear nothing more she had to say.

"Take the prisoner away!" ordered Powhatan.

Pocahontas couldn't bear to watch. Nakoma came out of the crowd and put her arm around her.

"I should have stayed in the village," Pocahontas told her, wiping her eyes.

"It's not your fault," said Nakoma.

"Yes, it is," said Pocahontas. "Kocoum was just coming to protect me. If I hadn't gone out there . . ."

"No, Pocahontas," said Nakoma. Her voice was shaking. "*I* sent Kocoum after you."

"What!" gasped Pocahontas.

"I was so worried," said Nakoma. "I didn't want you to get hurt. I thought I was doing the right thing."

Pocahontas gently touched her friend's cheek.

"All this happened because of me," she said. "And now, because of me, John is going to die."

Her eyes were brimming with tears.

"I need to see him, Nakoma," she said. "One last time."

Nakoma took Pocahontas by the hand.

"Come with me," she said. "I know where they took him."

She led Pocahontas across the village to a secluded hut. Two guards at the doorway stopped them.

Nakoma spoke up. "Pocahontas wants to look into the eyes of the man who killed Kocoum."

The guards, not sure, looked at each other.

"Are you going to deny the wishes of the daughter of the Chief?" Nakoma asked them.

They stepped aside and let Pocahontas in.

John was sitting on the ground tied to a post. The tiny room was lit by a torch stuck into the dirt floor.

"Pocahontas!" he said, surprised to see her.

Pocahontas threw her arms around his neck.

"I'm so sorry," she whispered.

"For what?" said John. He tried to smile. "I've got out of worse scrapes than this. Can't think of any right now, but. . . ."

Tears streamed down Pocahontas' face.

"It would have been better if we had never met," she said, "none of this would have happened."

"Pocahontas, look at me," he said. "I had to meet you. Because if I hadn't, I'd still be the man I was."

"What do you mean?" asked Pocahontas.

"You've changed me," he told her. "If I'd never

61

known you, I would have no idea how precious life can be."

Pocahontas brushed back her tears.

"I was so foolish," she said, "I thought our love could make the whole world bright." Sadly, she shook her head. "I never knew that fear and hate could be so strong. But still, my heart knows that we were right."

Nakoma poked her head inside. "We'd better go."

Pocahontas sobbed and clutched John's sleeve. "I can't leave you."

"You never will," he said. "No matter what happens to me. I'll always be with you. *Forever*."

Thomas stumbled wildly from the moonlit woods.

"Help!" he shouted bursting through the settlement gate. "Somebody, help! Help! Help!"

Carrying a lantern, Lon came running up to him. "Easy, lad! What is it?"

While more men clustered about him, Thomas stopped to catch his breath. Then he cried out, "It's Smith! The Indians got him! Captured him. Carried him off!"

"How many were there?" asked Ben. "Where'd they take him?"

"They headed north," Thomas told him. "There were at least a dozen of them."

Lon shook his fist. Ratcliffe was right. They are savages!

"We've got to save him!" cried Thomas. "He'd do the same for any of us."

"He's right," said Ben, "We've got to do something."

Overhearing the commotion, Governor Ratcliffe came out of his house.

"It's perfect, Wiggins!" he whispered. "I couldn't have planned this better myself. The gold is as good as mine!"

Ratcliffe strode up to the men. "And so we shall rescue Smith!" he boomed.

"I told you those Indians couldn't be trusted," he said. "Smith tried to befriend them, and look what they've done!"

Ratcliffe unsheathed his sword and held it high.

"It's time to rescue our courageous comrade," he cried into the night. "Gather your weapons. At daybreak we attack!"

In his village not far away, Chief Powhatan had just cried out these same words.

While it was still dark, Pocahontas paddled towards the heart of the forest. As soon as the canoe slid into the glade, she leapt out and ran to Grandmother Willow.

"They're going to kill him at sunrise!" she cried.

Grandmother Willow was horrified. "You have to stop them!"

Pocahontas put her hands to her mouth and shook her head. "I can't."

"Child," said Grandmother Willow, "you must not turn away from your path. Remember your dream."

"I don't know which way to turn," said Pocahontas. She sobbed. "I feel so lost."

Just then Meeko raced up into the tree. In a moment, he was at Pocahontas's side, nudging her arm.

Then she felt a little tug on her arm. Surprised, she found Meeko sitting next to her. He was holding up something shiny. It was John's compass.

Pocahontas smiled sadly. "Thank you, Meeko," she said, taking it from him. In the dim light she watched the needle spin and remembered John's words. "It tells you how to find your way when you get lost . . ."

She stopped short. She noticed something for the first time. The needle was shaped like a tiny arrow!

"Spinning arrow," she breathed.

Excited, she held it up.

"It's the arrow from your dream!" said Grandmother Willow.

"I was right!" Pocahontas cried. "This is my path!"

The compass face glinted in the first rays of early light. Pocahontas looked to the glowing eastern sky. The sun was rising.

"It's sunrise!" she gasped. "I'm too late!"

"Have faith, Child," said Grandmother Willow. "Let the spirits of the Earth guide you."

As Pocahontas gazed up at Grandmother Willow, a gentle wind began to flow. It ruffled her hair. Feeling its comforting presence around her, she thought of her mother and smiled.

Quickly, the wind picked up speed and the compass needle began to spin wildly. It spun faster and faster. Then all at once it stopped.

"It's pointing east," said Pocahontas, "to the sunrise!"

As swift as a lightning bolt, the wind cleared an opening for her through the forest.

"You know your path, Child," said Grandmother Willow. "Now follow it!"

Pocahontas raced through the shadowy trees. As she ran, the wind stayed with her, pushing steadily at her back. There was so little time. She had to get home – before it was too late!

Governor Ratcliffe stood to attention in the centre of Jamestown. Smiling broadly, he watched the rim of gold peak above the horizon. The day had come at last. The day they would wipe out the Indians. And, while they were at it, if they managed to rescue Smith – well, that would be good too.

He turned to face his battallion of waiting men.

"Onward!" he ordered, waving his sword in the air.

At once, the settlers marched into the forest, hacking at the trees and bushes that stood in their way.

On top of a high plateau, Chief Powhatan, too, was watching the rising sun. He knew the sun was dawning on his people's brightest day. The day of their victory over the invaders!

But first, there was something else to attend to.

He turned to the villagers. They were all standing in a semi-circle near the plateau's edge. In the centre of the circle lay a stone slab.

"Bring out the prisoner," he demanded.

Two warriors brought John out. They pushed him onto the stone slabs and held him down. Powhatan raised his war club.

At that moment, Ratcliffe and his men burst out of the trees at the foot of the plateau and raised their muskets.

"NO!" screamed Pocahontas, streaking past them.

She raced up to her father and threw herself across John.

Shocked by her actions, Ratcliffe's men halted.

"Hey mate," Ben whispered to Lon. "What the heck's going on?"

Astounded, Chief Powhatan lowered his arm. "Pocahontas!"

She looked up at him. "If you kill him," she said, "you'll have to kill me, too."

"Daughter!" ordered the Chief. "Stand back!"

"I won't," Pocahontas said, still holding onto John. "I love him, Father."

Chief Powhatan was stunned.

"Look around you," said Pocahontas. "This is where the path of hatred has brought us."

Powhatan could see the white men positioned at the edge of the forest. His own warriors, arrows poised in their bows, were looking to him for orders.

His daughter's next words rang in his ears:

"This is the path *I* choose, Father. What will yours be?"

As she spoke, the wind stirred in the surrounding trees. Leaves of green and scarlet and gold floated about everyone's head. As the wind swirled gently around Powhatan's shoulders, his eyes grew misty. Then standing tall, he raised his voice for all to hear.

"My daughter speaks with a wisdom beyond her years," he said. "We have all come here with anger in our hearts. But she comes with courage and understanding. It is that spirit that will guide us to a place of peace."

He turned to the warriors.

"Release the prisoner!"

All the warriors, stirred by the power of Powhatan's words, lowered their weapons.

At that, Governor Ratcliffe yelled, "Now's our chance, men! Fire!"

Thomas, moved by the warriors' actions, immediately stepped forward and lowered his musket. One by one, his comrades followed.

"Fine!" said Ratcliffe. "I'll settle this myself!"

Before anyone could move, he grabbed a musket and aimed straight at Chief Powhatan.

In an instant, John threw himself at Powhatan and knocked him out of the way. But Ratcliffe had already pulled the trigger. The musket exploded and John fell to the ground.

"He's shot John!" cried Thomas.

Enraged, Ratcliffe's men closed in on him.

"Put him in chains!" cried Thomas.

"Smith stepped right into it!" the governor protested. "It's his own fault. You saw it yourself!" He broke away from their grasp and ran, tripping over Meeko and Percy.

"I'll see that you are all hanged for this!" Ratcliffe shouted, as they recaptured him and put him in chains.

"Gag him as well," added Thomas.

He hurried over to John's side. Pocahontas, crying softly, was holding him in her arms. He was still alive.

11

In less than a week, the *Susan Constant* was loaded and ready for the voyage back to England.

Just before the ship set sail, Thomas helped to carry John down to the shore. Gently, the men placed the stretcher in a shady spot under the trees.

John smiled weakly at Thomas.

"I'm glad you're staying behind," he said. "When the new settlers arrive, you can help . . ." Then he began to cough.

"I'll get you some water," Thomas said.

He hurried over to a rain barrel and filled the tin dipper. Ben and Lon joined him.

"How's Smith holding up?" asked Ben.

"He should be all right," said Thomas, "as long as he gets back to England."

A commotion erupted near the settlement gate.

"Look," said Lon, "here they come with Ratcliffe."

The governor struggled vainly at his chains while

he was loaded into a small boat and rowed out to the ship.

Thomas held John's head up while he drank.

"Make sure you tell them back home what has happened here," said Thomas.

John nodded. "I will."

"We'd better get you on board," said Ben, "before the tide goes out."

John held up his hand. "No, not yet. Pocahontas said she'd be here."

Wincing, he pushed himself up on his elbow and looked towards the forest. Then he smiled. "She's coming," he said, falling back on the stretcher. "Thomas, go and meet her."

Pocahontas had reached the edge of the clearing. Chief Powhatan and Nakoma were at her side.

"Does he have to go?" Pocahontas asked Thomas.

"Going back is his only chance," Thomas said, kindly. "He'll die if he stays here."

For several moments Pocahontas stared out at the river. Nakoma put her arm round her.

"I know what you are thinking," she said. "But remember, dear Pocahontas, the fighting has stopped because of you. Who knows what will happen if you leave?"

Pocahontas watched her people coming from the village. They were carrying blankets and baskets of

71

corn for the white men. "This is the first peace since the sailing ship arrived," she thought.

She went to John. Kneeling, she stroked his forehead.

"I have something for you," she said. She tucked a small leather pouch in his shirt. "It is powdered bark from Grandmother Willow. It will help with the pain."

"What pain?" asked John. "I've had worse pain than this. Can't think of when right now, but . . ." Then he shivered.

Chief Powhatan removed his mantle and laid it over John.

John smiled. "Thank you," he said.

Flit buzzed over and landed on John's finger.

"I thought you didn't like strangers," said John, weakly.

He watched as Meeko and Percy scrambled up to Pocahontas and dropped something in her lap.

"My mother's necklace!" said Pocahontas. "Thank you!"

John patted the two animals and smiled.

"Will you come with me?" he asked Pocahontas, taking her hand.

Pocahontas looked up at her father.

"You must choose your own path," he told her.

Tears streamed down Pocahontas' face.

John knew her decision. "Then I will stay here with you," he said.

Pocahontas shook her head. "No," she said, "you have to go back."

"But I can't leave you!" said John.

"You will never leave me," Pocahontas said. "No matter what happens, I'll always be with you. *Forever*."

Pocahontas ran to the edge of the cliff. Alone, she watched as The *Susan Constant* moved away from her, its huge white sails billowing in the wind down the wide river to the waters that had no end.